what a day . . .

# What a Day!

*Never have another bad day*

by Seran Wilkie

*[handwritten: To: Michelle, No more Bad Days! Seran 3/2/06]*

*WME*
Books

a division of
*Windsor Media Enterprises, LLC*

Rochester, New York
USA

what a day ... *What a Day!*
*Never have another bad day*

ISBN 0-9765304-3-0

Project Editor: Karen Monaco
Cover Design: Karin Marlett Choi
Page Layout/Design: Tom Collins

Published by:
WME Books
Windsor Media Enterprises, LLC
Rochester, New York
USA

Available online at: www.WMEBooks.com
as well as other booksellers and distributors worldwide

**Special Sales:**
This and other WME Books titles are available at special
discounts for bulk purchases, for use in sales promotions or
premiums. Special editions, including personalized covers,
excerpts of existing books, and corporate imprints, can be
created in large quantities for special needs or projects.

For more information, please contact:

Special Book Orders
Windsor Media Enterprises, LLC
150 Lucius Gordon Drive
West Henrietta, NY 14586

info@wmebooks.com

# Acknowledgments

I would like to thank all my children and their families for their contributions to this book, including help with writing, editing, ideas, photos, and graphics.

I especially want to recognize the help of Karen Monaco, who edited the manuscript and skillfully captured its essence in her original drafts of the before and after story sections.

I also would like to thank Yvonne DiVita, Tom Collins, and everyone at WME Books for coming to my rescue and helping me give the final push to the birth of this book.

Finally, thanks to all of my friends — you know who you are — for being part of my life lesson.

— Seran

# Contents

# Foreword

Foreword

This book is written in response to requests made by friends and clients.

My husband and I have gathered 'bad day' scenarios on our yearly trips to Cancun, Mexico. It's funny, but a lot of vacationers from all over and different ages were more than willing to share their 'bad days.'

Most of us believe that bad days are caused by something outside of ourselves. Then, once it starts, it almost always gets worse.

# I believe that bad days *do not* have to exist.

Most of us have listened to our grandparents and parents talking about their bad days. We've had our share and now we're passing them on like family heirlooms to our children.

They say, "Bad days happen. Just grin and bear it."

I say, *"Make me."*

—**Seran Wilkie**

# Preface: Before Story

Ask anyone and they'll tell you they have had good days and bad days. But what or who has taught that individual what constitutes a bad or good day? Or, more importantly, where does one learn that "good" or "bad" days even exist?

The answer to that is simple—we modeled the example from those who raised us. We can all picture authority figures in our childhood who said they had a bad day or were in a bad mood, and in turn, we learned that when certain things happen that we dislike, we should react negatively.

But a more difficult question is how can bad days be eliminated so that we can find more happiness than we have now?

While this may seem nearly impossible, by altering how you perceive each and every situation that comes your way, it will become a reality. Although unpleasant events will undoubtedly still occur in one's life, it is the perception and reaction to that event that will forever change your state of happiness, and eliminate what you now consider to be a "bad" day.

We have been trained by society to have certain psychological and physical responses to what we view as stressful situations. Being late to work, spilling a cup of coffee on your lap before a big presentation, not getting a promotion, and even a terrible car accident are all events that society says are bad and unfortunate within different degrees. But, I challenge you to think differently.

By thinking negative thoughts, your body automatically tenses up, you become anxious, and energy is expelled on this uncontrollable event. In essence, precious energy is wasted — energy that could have been utilized to be a better parent or a more efficient manager.

Although no one will disagree that any of the above events are unpleasant, it is impossible to change them once they have occurred. The only thing you can control is how you choose to respond to these events.

The key to recapturing this wasted energy is learning to de-program what society has taught you about reacting to life's stressful situations. By training your body to handle unpleasant events in a more positive way, physically and psychologically, it is possible to harness this lost energy into something productive. Just as you learned to curse or get upset when something happens that you dislike, you can unlearn this response and train your body to react in a positive way.

This is not to say you will teach yourself to feel joy when you lose your job or when you are frustrated with your children; rather, you will automatically avoid expending unnecessary energy on becoming upset when the inevitable unpleasant event occurs. You will train yourself to bypass the frustration, anxiety, and anger that is quite simply a waste, diverting that saved energy into solving the problem at hand or getting over the situation you dislike.

The following story tells about "Guy," a manager having a "bad day," one that almost anyone can relate to in one way or another. While reading, take note of how much time Guy spends thinking about how terrible his life and day is, and in turn, how much energy he expends responding negatively to the events.

Consider, just for a little while, what would happen if Guy looked at each seemingly "bad" event differently. Ask yourself how his perception of his day would change, along with his level of happiness and overall sense of self-worth. Reflect on how such a simple change might replace his feelings of angst and emptiness with a stockpile of positive energy that can make him the best person he can be.

# 1 - Why me?

Whoosh. Shhhhush. Blissful silence again. *A toilet flush. Yes. Definitely a toilet flush. That would mean that the children are awake. If the kids are up and getting ready, then - uh oh.*

Guy reached his arm out and pulled the clock up to his half-lidded eyes. The clock challenged him with a blinking 3:15. He closed his eyes. *If it's 3:15, who's going to the bathroom? Why did I wake up? Did I leave a light on? Why is it so bright in the room?*

And with that last question, Guy woke up. ***Why does this have to happen to me today?*** His senses were starting to come around and the sounds around the house were becoming more obvious - footsteps all around, doors and drawers opening and shutting.

"Stupid alarm clock," Guy muttered.  He threw off the blankets, rolled out of bed and made a beeline for the master bathroom.

"Maggie," he spoke sternly.

Guy's wife was still motionless on the bed. The comforter was all bundled around her with only her brown hair flowing out the top like a chocolate ice cream cone.

"Something's wrong with the alarm clock," he said from the bathroom as he reached in and twisted the faded plastic shower controls. The cold tile floor shocked his feet.

Silence.

Maggie obviously did not want to get up this morning either.

"Maggie, I'm going to be late for my meeting," he added, slightly annoyed as he looked at the clock on the bathroom wall. *Dammit!* ***How many times do I have to wake her up? If I have to get up, she has to get up!***

"Maggie! Wake up! It's 7:15 and I'm already late!" Guy twisted out of his pajamas and jumped into the shower.

"Yow!" he shouted as the cold water hit him in the chest. He hadn't waited long enough for the hot water pipes to warm up.

*"What's wrong?"* asked Maggie as she stumbled into the bathroom doorway.

"Nothing," Guy huffed.

The hot water poured over him as he washed his short cropped hair. He quickly massaged the soap around the sags and bulges of his slightly worn out body. Instead of feeling refreshed he felt less than half-awake and miserable. At times like this during his childhood his mom always used to say, "Looks like someone woke up on the wrong side of the bed and *when you wake up grumpy you stay grumpy all day*."

Guy left the shower with a towel and headed for the dresser. He pulled open a drawer and reached into empty air. Guy frowned.

"Maggie! Where's my underwear?"

"Your underwear? It's in your drawer where it always is." She didn't sound surprised. She sounded irritated.

"No... it's... not," he replied, pronouncing each word separately as he reached in again. "Why don't I have any underwear in the drawer?"

"If you want clean underwear do your own wash," she replied, eyeing the dirty clothes hamper. "Or better yet, wear one of mine. I heard that some men like wearing women's underwear." She was grinning.

"*I hate it when things are not where they should be.* I'll just wear a pair from yesterday," Guy responded. He wasn't going to dignify her statement and started towards the hamper. He reached underneath the lid and rummaged through the clothes.

"Why are all of these wet?" he asked. He was beginning to have a fit. "There are no dry clothes in the hamper!  Why is the hamper all wet?  I can't believe this!"  He was shaking some soggy underwear in his hand accusingly.

"Oh," Maggie replied while stepping into her bathrobe. "I threw some dish towels in there last night. They must have soaked through. Anyway, *I've got to cook breakfast* for the kids before they leave." She paused pityingly as she opened the hallway door. "*Poor baby...* I'll make you some toast and put your coffee in a thermos so you can drink it on the way to work."

She walked out and shut the door. The sound of her footsteps barely started retreating before the kids began calling out for her.

Guy frowned and stared into space. The kids. He loved them but they were so demanding. *They were always first. Why do I always have to be last?*  Sometimes he felt like they only wanted his paycheck. Guy shook off his self-pity.

"So I can either wear wet, dirty underwear or clean women's underwear." He rubbed his bristled face. "What a way to start the day."

Guy reached into his wife's drawer and grabbed a pair of underwear. He stretched it out in front of him. It was made of some satin red material that had lace around the edges. He pictured himself in a car accident and a bunch of nurses laughing as doctor asked him questions. The underwear went back into the drawer. Guy gritted his teeth, put on his pants and stepped back into the bedroom to finish dressing.

While he was completing the knot on his tie for the second time, Maggie opened the door and poked her head in. "So what did you choose?" She smirked and shut door again.

"Thanks for nothing," he replied as the door shut. He was in no mood to be the butt of Maggie's joke.

In the mirror he looked like any other middle-aged working stiff: white oxford shirt, tie, pressed pants, and dark socks, except for the lack of underwear. Hey, he had a job, a marriage, two children, two cars and a roof over their heads. *What am I complaining about? I should be content.* He tried to smile to himself in the mirror but it came out weak.

*"Loser,"* he muttered to himself as he opened the hallway door.

what a day ...

# 2 - I just knew it

The kitchen was business as usual. This morning, Maggie was stirring a pan of eggs at the stove, her back to the center of the room. She was in her blue bathrobe and red slippers, completely contrasting the country kitchen decor.

Guy's 12-year-old son, John, was sitting at the table in the middle of the kitchen, reading a skateboarding magazine and shoving a spoonful of something into his mouth. Irene, his 6-year-old princess, was sitting on the other side of the table with her shoulder length brown hair all piled on top of her head, waiting impatiently for Maggie.

"Mom..." whined Irene. She impatiently rocked the chair back and forth on its back legs. Children were innocent but demanding.

This was a suburban jackpot: Everyone at their posts ... the smell of eggs, toast, coffee ... kids eating breakfast. All they needed now was a dog barking.

Guy shifted moods like a car shifting gears in New York City traffic. Now he was touched by the scene in front of him and wanted to say something nice. For just a moment, he forgot about work and felt happy. Then he looked at his watch and realized he was in trouble. Not only was he late, but traffic was always worse as the morning drew on. A quick panic washed over him.

"Mooomm, " Irene blasted again as if she were Guy's reality alarm clock. "I'm waiiittting, Mommm." She dragged out the words and kept repeating them as she hopped up and down in her chair making it sound like she was on horseback.

Guy exploded.

"*Irene, you have to wait.* Can't you see that Dad's late and he needs his breakfast first?"

He regretted his outburst immediately.

Maggie whipped around scowling, and then turned her back once more. So much for her happy mood, too.

Irene gave Guy a pouting look that started to turn into her I'm-about-to-cry-and-give-you-something-to-really-be-sorry-about act.

Guy kept his stern face on. He thought about going on the offensive and telling Irene not to cry. Then he thought about apologizing to his daughter and trying to calm her down.

"Whoops. *Gotta go.* Love you guys."

Guy grabbed a piece of toast from Johnny's plate and a second from Irene's plate. The kids didn't have time to complain because he grabbed his briefcase, thermos and cell phone, kissed Maggie on the cheek and opened the front door in one fluid motion. Why confront, when you can run?

Once safe outside the door, he noticed that the sky was completely overcast and the wind was gusting heavily. The weatherman had forecasted a slim chance of rain but mostly sunshine. *There must be some sort of rule that Mondays increase bad weather odds.* Movement on the driveway next door caught his eye.

Art was standing at the end of his driveway, with a newspaper in his hand. In Guy's opinion, Art was a fat, lazy old coot who liked to complain. He liked to complain a lot. Art was always complaining about his ex-wife and that his two sons lived with her in a separate house. Today, Art wore a brown terry cloth robe – that just barely closed around his waist – and dirty white socks that didn't match. He was shuffling his feet and glancing up and down the street. It looked like he was ready to rant about the placement of his paper again.

Guy had no time for Art. He pretended not to see him and fumbled for the car keys in his pocket while opening the driver's door. A strong gust of wind caught the door at the same time causing it to fly open and hit him in the leg. BAM!

"Oww!!" Guy grabbed his leg while cursing to himself and involuntarily dropping everything.

THUD. BONK!

The briefcase and thermos bounced and rolled, respectively, on the pavement. His cell phone made a sharp cracking noise.

"Damn. I swear."

Guy immediately forgot about the pain in his leg. Please don't be broken. He picked up the phone, flipped open the lid, and stared at the display. The power was on. The bars and buttons lit up. He placed the phone in his jacket and patted it reassuringly.

After taking a minute to gather his composure and his briefcase, Guy reached for the car door again.

"You alright? It looks like you're having a bad day already."

Guy threw his things in the car before looking up. It was Art and he was grinning.

"Sounded like you really banged your leg good," Art said with emphasis. He wasn't being mean to Guy. Actually, Art treated Guy like he was one of his sons, but nicer.

"Bad luck with this weather for you, huh? I'll just bet my boys are gettin' all beat up at my ex's house. You know that stupid wife of mine raised my two boys to be some sort of klutzes."

"Yeah. Hey there, Art."

*I should talk to him, but I'm really late already.* But, Guy didn't want to be impolite. He started explaining that he had an important meeting this morning, and the next thing he knew, he was complaining about his clothes.

"All I'm asking for are some clean freaking clothes. Is that just too much to ask?" Guy waved his arms up and down in frustration.

"Yeah," Art agreed. "You're right about that. I feel the same way. All I ask for is for the paper to be delivered on time. Is that too much to ask? People nowadays. They just don't take pride in their work. They just want to rush, rush, rush. And what the hell are they rushing to? I'll tell you what they're rushing to." Art paused to pick at something lodged in between his front teeth. He looked at Guy very seriously. "Nothing. They're all in a hurry to go do diddly."

Guy shook a concerned look off of his face. What the hell was Art talking about? He looked at his watch and became concerned again. Art wasn't going to stop complaining and Guy had to cut this session short.

"Speaking of rushing, I really gotta go." Guy said as he sat in the car and closed the door.

"Sure, sure. Just watch out for all those crazies out there." Art walked away abruptly.

The drive to work was just as he had expected — bumper to bumper traffic, nauseating gas fumes and idiots swerving all over the road. *It never failed.* After Guy decided to change lanes, the car in front of him would slow down. He pulled out his cell phone to let work know he'd be late for the meeting. Guy dialed in the number and pressed send. Nothing happened. He was not surprised. It was Monday after all. He pressed the send button several times before throwing the phone down in the passenger seat.

"The right lane is for slower traffic," he shouted at any car that braked in front of him. It began to sound like a chant. *How did all these people happen to know that he was already late for his meeting today? Why did this always have to happen to him? What was wrong with his cell phone? And what the hell was Art complaining about? He doesn't have to go to a stupid meeting for a stupid boss. No kids at home demanding attention.*

Guy decided to turn the radio on to settle his nerves, but there was no music. Every station this morning had either commercials blasting drugs for impotence or a jockey acting like some crazed monkey on the mike. "I just don't understand how they pay people for that," he said to himself. "I could get on the radio, do the same junky routine and get paid thousands of dollars instead of having to suffer through this traffic everyday for a stupid meeting."

He switched off his radio. The honking cars, the smell of exhaust, smog in the air. All of it was making him more and more irate.

"Yes, this is WGUY, the Why Guy talking to you this lousy morning, blah blah bub blaooyey. And I've got a special request for all of you drivers on highway." He pointed at the drivers around him. "Hey! When you see a brown, four-door Buick on the road this morning, with a middle aged white male at the wheel, why don't you pull in front of him and hit the brakes? Yeah!"

Guy hit the steering wheel with his imaginary microphone.

"We've got a real winner here who's late for another meeting and why don't we just try to push his buttons a little bit more?" Guy paused and saw his exit coming up ahead. "As a matter of fact, why don't we see how many cars we can pile in front of him before he can exit the freeway?"

He was determined not to let anymore cars in front of him, but had to tap his brakes as a tractor-trailer switched on its blinkers and pulled in front of him.

Guy slammed on the horn.

"Unbelievable!" he shouted.

*Why not expect a jumbo jet to come careening out of the sky and make an emergency landing in front of him?* He tried to comfort himself. *Well, at least I'm not slamming on my horn and screaming out the window like Art does.*

At the office parking lot Guy found one parking space left at the far back corner. *How is it possible for the whole lot to be full?* He switched the engine off. *What if I arrived three minutes later? Would there be no parking spaces for me? How am I supposed to work if there are no parking spaces left!*

Guy grabbed his briefcase and slammed the door. He kicked the front tire to retaliate against the day and then looked around to see if anyone was watching. After straightening out his shirt, he limped towards the entrance.

# 3 - Can it get any worse?

"Good morning, sir," came a voice from behind the receptionist's desk.

Guy didn't recognize the voice.

There had been six receptionists in the past two years. The receptionist this month was some young girl possibly in her early twenties with short blonde curly hair. She was wearing a tight pink blouse covered by white knit sweater jacket. Guy felt she was just a little too heavy to be wearing such a provocative outfit. The girl was chewing a wad of gum. She waved at him and flashed a toothy smile.

*Why don't these people just grin, bear it and do their jobs?* He thought to himself. *I've been with this company for 12 years. I don't complain and then just quit my job every 6 months. What is with people these days? Are they just too good for everything? **Am I the only one who has to stick with a lousy job?***"

Guy barely managed a half smile.

"Sure. Good morning, right?" he started toward the half-closed elevator.

"Wait," he gasped. He leaned forward to hit the up button as fast as he could but slipped and accidentally hit the down button. Correcting himself, Guy hit the up button repeatedly while tapping his foot furiously.

When the doors opened, Guy rushed into an empty elevator and pressed the "close doors" button.

He started to plan his run to the meeting and then stopped.

*With my luck I'll walk in on a full meeting as someone is making a joke about me. Then they'll hear me give a lame excuse and think I'm an idiot.*

He was already feeling humiliated.

The elevator doors opened and Guy stepped out. The hallway was poorly lit and empty boxes and containers full of loose paper were all over the floor. Nobody was walking the halls. He squinted trying to make sense it all.

"What the ..." he mouthed. Then he remembered hitting the down button. He was in the basement. Guy stepped back into the elevator.

This day was really starting to piss him off.

The doors opened on the first floor and the receptionist waved at Guy again. Guy wanted to tell her to turn around and do her job, but he ignored her instead.

Mid-stride stepping out of the elevator on the second floor, Guy bumped right into his boss, Wade.

Wade was three years younger than Guy and managed to vault ahead because he had a business degree from an Ivy League school. Not to mention, Wade's father was friends with one of the vice presidents.

Again, Guy's briefcase made a thud as it hit the floor.

"Well. Good morning, Guy," said Wade as he straightened the tie underneath his suit jacket. "I guess you were not aware that we had a meeting first thing this morning?" Wade was looking down at Guy sternly.

"Uh, yes I was, Wade," Guy stammered, picking up his briefcase. *Don't mention the underwear.* "I had a problem with my alarm clock this morning, my cell phone wouldn't work, and traffic was un..."

"Well," Wade interrupted as if Guy wasn't even talking. "I also feel it safe to assume you did not get the message that our meeting was moved back an hour. I had trouble getting up this morning, too." Wade cracked a smile and slapped Guy on the shoulder. "Maybe a little coffee would do the trick. Why don't you make some, since the machine is empty? Then we can think about getting this meeting rolling."

Wade raised an empty mug in his left hand and handed it to Guy.

"Uh, sure." Guy said. *Yeah this is what I'm good for.* He switched his briefcase to his left hand and accepted the mug.

"No sugar or cream," Wade announced as he turned around and started down the hallway. "Thanks in advance."

That was Wade's trademark. He was always shooting off "Thanks in advance" like it was some sort of dapper thing to do. It was something he must have learned to say in manager's school. Guy thought it sounded stupid and it always made him angry. He wished he could just tell Wade to shut up. He couldn't understand how Wade managed to make him so upset.

Guy walked to his cubicle, shoved aside some papers with the mug and flipped his briefcase on top of the desk. He thought about hurling the mug across the room. Guy could barely think straight because he was so angry.

He wanted to shout, "Sure!  I'll make some coffee!  I may not get any real work done this morning but I will have made the coffee!"

It took him 5 minutes to calm down, and then he went to make the coffee.

The coffee machine was well utilized, a large silver bullet with multiple dings on the sides. The coffee it produced was miserable, but much less miserable than no coffee. "It's a good thing

I have twelve years of experience so I can make coffee for everyone," Guy grumbled as he dismantled the machine. The cup was full of grounds from the previous Friday. The smell reached out and almost pulled his stomach from his nose.

"Damn!  Would it kill someone to clean the machine after they take the last cup?" He threw the cup in the sink and picked up a spoon.

Now that the smell had been released from the coffee machine it had begun to wander into the hallway, attracting further victims.

"Hey, Guy! Whoa! How about cleaning that thing once a month?"

Guy swung around quickly on the linoleum surface with his slick shoes, gripping a spoon in his fist.

Lambert, known throughout the office as Lamb, (because he was always on the run) was smiling in a white shirt, red tie and brown pants. He was waving a white mug in his left hand as if in a toast. After seeing the look in Guy's eyes, he backed up a step, and kept the mug in front for defense.

"Whoa there. Have you got a permit for that thing?" Lambert prodded.

Lambert and Guy were pretty good friends. Occasionally they would meet after work for drinks and talk about how tough things were. Not a lot in common, but they always complained about their jobs at least once a day.

Guy saw Lambert back up and relaxed his grip on the spoon.

*"I am having a bad day."* Guy sighed loudly and tried to salvage the situation. He turned around and went back to his assignment.

"One of those days, huh?" Lambert asked as he cautiously peered around the coffee nook.

"Let's just say I'm absolutely sure it's Monday," Guy replied. "And I'm ready to go home." He pulled out a large brown can and used his spoon to dole out coffee grounds.

"Well, don't worry," Lambert offered. "After our marathon meeting this morning it'll feel like Tuesday or maybe even Wednesday." He paused. "But, now I'm going back to my desk, where it's safe."

Guy smirked in spite of himself. He took comfort that they would all feel miserable in the meeting together. He didn't have to turn around to know that Lambert left. Who could stay with that awful smell?

# 4 - The setup

Fifteen people filed into the small room around a large oval wooden table. They tried to get themselves comfortable and chattered to each other as Wade called the meeting to order.

"Well, it's Monday again," Wade began.

It was a widely held belief that Monday meetings were only held to reinforce the obvious. It was also obvious that Wade never prepared for any of these meetings. Not exactly an inspiring situation.

"So here we are again at the table ready to discuss our objectives for this week, the next week and the rest of this month."

Guy stared at the table. Everyone was anticipating a long and painful meeting. From the erratic arm waving and pointing, it was easy to determine that not only was Wade floundering, but this was going to be yet another complete waste of all of their time.

"So I'd like to say that last week was fairly productive," Wade continued. "Though we are definitely in need of major improvements or some new projects. Does anybody have any ideas to put on our plate for this month or the following?" He sipped from his mug that Guy had filled.

Guy had several ideas that might raise productivity but he was afraid to speak up. All the way from middle school through college, he could never be the first to speak up in dead silence. He was afraid of all the attention and sounding stupid.

***Come on stupid! Say something.*** He stared very hard at the table, upset that he couldn't take advantage of this situation, but trying to blend into the woodwork.

"Guy. You got something in mind?"

He heard his name and took a couple seconds to replay the full question. He hadn't planned on being asked to divulge an idea. He wasn't mentally ready.

Under pressure, Guy started to mumble ideas disjointedly. "Increased improvement. Yes, several areas ... of change to ... well ... I mean ..." He paused.

Wade was leaning forward with a questioning look on his face. Guy could tell he had everyone's attention and a glimmer of hope crept into his head. This was a chance to step up.

"What was that, Guy?" Wade prompted, tapping a pen on his head. "Sounds like you're stockpiling some great ideas over there."

The room was silent. Guy could almost hear the sweat coming out his pores. Everyone was leaning forward in their chairs in anticipation, but with a puzzled look on all of their faces. He took a deep breath of air filled with the fragrance of stale coffee and aftershave. Success was within his reach. And why not? He had waited long enough for this good thing to come.

Guy quickly leaned his chair forward again and prepared to lay out his ideas for improvement. *Maybe I'll pull this off.* He crossed his fingers.

Then, the new receptionist walked through the door.

# 5 - Cheated again

All eyes in the room shifted from Guy and waited for the receptionist to speak.

She smiled at everyone and then chewed her gum. The group was not going to successfully intimidate her to hurry up. She made eye contact with Guy and then Wade.

"I'm sorry to interrupt, Wade," she said apologetically toward the front of the room. "But I have Guy's mother on the phone and she says it's extremely urgent. It can't wait." She popped a bubble at the end for emphasis.

The sound of fourteen pressed pants turning on vinyl coated chair cushions filled the room. The spotlight was on Guy once again in a mixture of pitying looks and delighted grins. He couldn't speak. What could he say? He didn't understand what just happened. *Did that new receptionist just tell everyone that my mom called? At such an important moment? When I was just about to prove to everyone how valuable I am to the company? Was she sure it was my mom? Aren't there any other Guys working at this company?*

Guy left his mouth open while he continued thinking. ***Can't I ever get a break?*** *This was a major lose-lose situation. If I tell the secretary I'll call my mother later, that might look like I don't care about family, and how can I be counted on to take care of my team with that attitude? On the other hand if I leave the room, I'll lose this chance to speak up.*

"Guy?" Wade was tapping his head again with the pen. The receptionist was waiting impatiently with her hands on the hem of her slightly bulging skirt.

Guy realized he was in trouble. He knew he had to take the call but he didn't want to leave his chair. *Why does this have to happen to me?* Guy was still struggling. *I'm a good employee. I pay taxes. I don't steal things.* He couldn't think of anything intelligent to say and everyone was expecting him to do something.

Guy got up quickly, swung around and stole towards the door. "I'd better take this call," he said to the office behind him. "Sorry about the interruption. I'll be back as soon as I can."

Guy stormed through the hallways back to his cubicle. He was thoroughly annoyed. "This had better be important!" he said aloud when he reached his area. He pulled out his chair and sat down. Surrounded by stacks of paper and projects, the red transfer light on his phone blinked like a beacon. She was waiting. He wanted to punch the phone, but picked up the receiver instead.

"Okay. What?" he said, struggling to keep his frustration in check. "It's Guy. What's the emergency? Are you all right?" It suddenly dawned on Guy that it could be a medical emergency and he was upset with himself for being selfish.

"Guy! Guy I ... it was in the basement ... well, I was just going to do some ... and the ..." She was clearly panicking.

"Mom. I don't understand. Start over. What's the problem? Tell me what the problem is."

"Oh, Guy," she whispered. She drew in a large breath. "It was horrible. I was doing some wash in the basement because your father was running out of clean clothes. Honestly I don't understand how he can have so many dirty clothes without telling me."

"Mom," Guy interrupted impatiently. "Enough about the clothes already! What's wrong with the basement? Are you all right? Was somebody else down there?"

"Not somebody. Something." She gasped for air again. "Guy, as I was throwing your father's underwear in the washer, something was squirming in my hand!"

Guy hissed inwardly and shut his eyes. This was clearly not a medical emergency but if she didn't get to the point soon, he was going to have an aneurysm.

"Guy, I felt the squirming and I threw it down. It was a mouse! Guy! I had a mouse crawling all over my hands! All over your father's underwear! That mouse must have been in our bedroom. Oh, Guy! The dirty squirming thing is still in the basement!" She was hysterical. "Your father is out playing golf all day. Of all the days, I swear he has to pick today to go out! What do I do?"

Guy's mom had an irrational fear of mice. Mice paralyzed her. He wanted to say, "Don't be stupid. It's small. You're big. I'm in the middle of an important meeting." But it was pointless. Mickey Mouse made her squirm. Guy tried to take hold of the situation.

"Mom, are you still in the basement?"

"Yes," she replied timidly.

"Mom. Go upstairs. Make yourself a cup of tea and sit down and relax. I'll call an exterminator

and have them come out to the house right away."

It took a few more minutes of talking to get his mother to calm down, but eventually she released him from the phone. He took out a phone book and called several exterminators before he could find one that would visit the house that morning. At least that problem was solved.

Guy huffed. ***How can I be expected to handle everything?*** *I have to take care of my kids. I have to take care of my mom. I have to wake up my wife. I have to get my boss' coffee. Who am I, Superman? How the hell am I supposed to do my job?*

"Oh damn! The meeting!" He threw himself out of his chair. His mind was whirling about how to enter the room while his legs were on autopilot. He was getting excited again about presenting his ideas to the group as he reached the meeting room door.

He knocked lightly on the door once and began an apology as he entered. "Hey. Sorry about ..."

Guy looked around the room and saw that all the chairs were empty. He looked at the door number to make sure he was in the right room. It was the same meeting room, but no one was there. What was going on? Guy looked at his watch. He wasn't on the phone long enough for the meeting to end. *He needed some answers.* He found Lambert in the hallway.

"Yeah, lucky us," Lambert began. "Only a couple minutes after you escaped, Wade was called out by that gum chewing secretary. The meeting was postponed till next week." He was smiling at Guy. "Some quick thinking there, getting your mom to call you out of the meeting. Is she alright?"

"Yeah. She's fine. Crisis averted. It was just a small family emergency." Guy cut the conversation short and retreated to his cubicle. He didn't want to talk about mice or underwear anymore. He wanted to be alone and he wanted this day to be over. He thought about people like his mother and Art who just wanted to waste his time when he had more important things to do.

He wasted the rest of the day pushing papers around his desk, and avoided making anymore situations. ***Guy was certain that he was under a big black cloud.*** He just had to grin and bear it. As soon as 5:00 rolled around he promptly evacuated the building with his briefcase.

# 6 - Homeward

6 Homeward

*Another miserable drive to end yet another
miserable day.* Guy threw himself into the car.
*At least I'll get to do what I want at home and
I'll finally have something under control.* He
pulled out of the parking lot and headed home. He
noticed that his thermos was still on the passenger
seat, but the coffee was now cold.

Guy reached his house in a customary state of
frustration after mentally berating some fifteen
drivers on his way home. "I hate this car," he
muttered as he kicked the door open. "I hate
driving. I hate drivers. *I'm sick and tired of being
stuck in this car everyday.*" This venting episode
was also becoming a custom.

*All I want to do now is to be left alone, have a drink, and relax before dinner. This is the least I deserve.* Guy even mustered a tired smile as he envisioned himself sitting in front of the TV, propped up on his recliner, with a nice cold drink in each hand.

He picked up his briefcase and thermos from the car, walked to the front door and turned the doorknob. No one welcomed him home as he entered.

"Hey. Anybody home?" Guy questioned.

In fact nobody seemed to be around. Then Guy heard Maggie from the dining room.

"Guy is that you? You're late. Hurry up and come and have dinner with us. Did you forget that I have to take your son to his concert tonight?" She was definitely irate.

There was no reward here. No recliner with drinks, no television, no smiling.

*What did I expect? I always get the short end of the stick.*

Guy trudged into the dining room and sat down without speaking. He was defeated. He'd forgotten about the concert. *Oh well, just chalk up another loss for me.* He scooped several spoonfuls of tuna casserole on his plate and began to eat without looking up.

Maggie, Johnny and Irene stared at him as he ate. There was a lot of tension in the air. Maggie was upset because he was late to dinner. John resented the fact that Guy always had an excuse to skip the concerts, which Guy honestly hated attending. And Irene was becoming upset because nobody was paying any attention to her. Only the sound of silverware clanking on dinner plates filled the room. He didn't care anymore.

"I really have to go now, Guy, " Maggie said wiping her face with a napkin. "We've got half an hour till the concert and Johnny has to get there early to warm up." She got up from the table, kissed Irene on the head, while Johnny moped towards the door.

"Good luck, John," Guy offered as they left. He shrugged at Maggie and mouthed, *"I'm sorry."* But he wasn't sure if she saw him.

 Guy slumped at the table and put his head down in front of him. He felt like a complete failure. As an employee, as a husband, as a father, even as a human being.

"Hey, Daddy?" Irene asked. "Do you want to watch TV with me?"

Guy didn't want to be angry with Irene. He smiled halfheartedly. "Thanks, but I think I'll just sit here for a little bit. Why don't you go watch TV for a little while?"

After Irene left, he went to the kitchen and poured himself a cup of coffee.

He just wanted to sit down and unwind, but he just couldn't get the day's events out of his head. What a perfectly lousy day. At least he wasn't dead.

He tried to figure out why he was having so many bad days now. *Seems like every other day is miserable. What the hell was going on?* Guy needed something to happen, something different. *Maybe we all need to go on a vacation.*

Something had to happen or Guy was going to burst into flames. He sat there in the kitchen in a daze.

what a day ...

# 7 - The faint sound of an alarm

"Daddy," Irene was standing in front of him with her flowered pajamas on. "Daddy, it's time for me to go to bed. Come on, Dad. It's time for bed." She sounded happy. She'd already forgotten about the tense dinner moments. She was still just a six-year-old.

*And why not? I'd love to be a kid again. I'd be happy to go to bed if I was her. She doesn't have to get up and face those idiot drivers just to go make lousy coffee.* Guy smiled at Irene with a dash of pity for himself.

"Of course, Honey. Let's go." He got up and took her tiny hand in his and they walked to her room. He always enjoyed this part of the day because the routine partially pulled him out of his world and into Irene's.

As she climbed under her pink covers she asked, "Daddy? Why are you mad?"

She couldn't have known he was just grumpy.

"I'm not mad, Irene. I just had a bad start this morning and it made the whole day go rotten." Guy didn't want to replay the whole day's events to his six-year-old daughter. She wouldn't understand. He wanted to keep her childhood intact from the disgusting harsh reality of the real world – the humiliation, the idiots who control you, the fumbling for a purpose for being.

He tried to simplify the day.

"Well, something happened to Daddy's alarm clock last night and Daddy woke up an hour later."

"Lucky Daddy!" Irene interrupted. She clasped her hands and beamed a smile that made obvious the loss of two teeth.

"Lucky Daddy?" Guy struggled to make a connection.

"Yep. You're lucky you got to sleep more than I did. I was really tired this morning."

Guy forced a smile. She was too young to see the bad side of this situation. She had a lot to learn.

"That's true. Yes, well I guess Daddy should be happy then. Good night, Honey." He kissed Irene and watched her close her eyes. A look of contentment fell across her face.

Irene's words lingered in his head as got himself ready for bed.

*Imagine being happy about waking up late. What a crazy idea.* Guy thought about it some more until he fell asleep.

what a day ...

# After Story

After taking a glimpse into Guy's day, it is obvious that a lot of things did not go as he had hoped. One may even agree with him when he says, "I have a reason to be upset."

However, you may change your mind if you look differently at what happened during Guy's day. In reality, there truly was no reason to be upset, for the frustration that came with reacting to the unpleasant events did absolutely nothing to improve any of them. His alarm clock still would not have gone off at the right time, traffic would have remained at the same level of congestion, and his mother still would have interrupted his meeting regardless of how he responded.

The majority of Guy's day was spent thinking about what a bad day he was having, leaving little time to be the best manager and father that he could be. When one views the situation in this manner, it seems ridiculous that someone would spend almost all of their time and energy of an entire day complaining and stressing about events beyond their control. But, I think it is safe to say that at one point in almost everyone's lives, they have spent a day doing exactly that.

Consider this idea that getting upset did not change any of the unpleasant events of the day for Guy and that precious energy was used up, but accomplished nothing for him – energy that could have been used to tackle the issues at hand.

How can one learn to avoid responding negatively when things do not happen to one's liking? Isn't it natural for someone to be cranky when they wake up late or when traffic is slow? The answer is no; it only seems natural to react this way, because society has taught you that it is.

There were several people during Guy's day who reaffirmed his belief that bad days do exist and he was having one. He remembered when his mother used to say "looks like someone woke up on the wrong side of the bed", his neighbor, Art, asked him if he was already having a bad day, and one of his friends at work asked him if he's having one of "those" days. At least three people either came to Guy's mind or he came in contact with assured him that there are good days and bad.

However, Guy dismissed the perspective of the one person who thought differently about his situation – his daughter, Irene. She considered her father to be lucky that he obtained extra rest that morning when he overslept.

Guy would agree that he did get a little more sleep, but he would be quick to argue that it caused him to have a "bad" day. He also couldn't let go of the tensions at dinner like Irene did: "She'd already forgotten about the tense dinner moments. She was just a six-year-old."

Believe it or not, taking on this six-year-old perspective actually would have done more good for Guy during his day than his own middle-aged view. This is because Irene's positive response and perspective is our true natural response to unpleasant situations, contrary to popular belief. Her innate ability to brush things off is the key to understanding how we can do the same thing and become much happier in the process.

Guy told himself that the way Irene looks at things will change after she realizes the "harsh reality of the real world: the humiliation, the idiots who control you, the fumbling for a purpose for being." He wants to maintain her childhood naiveté, delaying her "realization" that as far as most of the adult world is concerned, there is nothing good about sleeping late and everyone dwells on difficult moments and relationships after the moment has passed.

Although that is how most of society would see Guy's day, it doesn't have to be that way for you.

Eliminating bad days is simply becoming Irene again. Learning some new and complicated training method to get our bodies in sync isn't necessary. But if you want to make this change, you will need to *unlearn* what society has taught you about reacting to life's problems, large or small.

We already know how to respond in this positive way. It is just something we've forgotten. And, it is something easy to forget when almost every other person around you tells you differently. The key is to consciously return to that child-like state by changing how you perceive the world, modifying the language you use, and re-teaching your mind and body to do what you want to do when something unpleasant occurs.

Be good to yourself and devote some time out of your busy day to your own personal happiness.

The next time a stressful situation occurs, just consider some of the alternate perceptions in this book. Review the Author's note that follows and take a few minutes to think about the examples of alternate ways Guy might have reacted to the specific events in Chapter 1 of the story.

Then take a few more minutes to come up with your own viewpoints on the events listed from the rest of the chapters. Use the remaining pages as a workbook to help you apply and internalize the habit of "becoming Irene" when you need to get past an irritating event, or respond to a stressful situation. Become aware of how to recognize and protect yourself from the negative perspectives of those around you.

Make notes in the margins and write out your own alternate perspectives. Revisit Guy's story and your developing ideas on a regular basis and see how your responses evolve.

You will find that in time, your thought process, which has been clouded by a spider web of negativity and false truths, will become clear again, freeing up your precious energy to be a more effective employee, spouse, or parent, and eventually, a happier person.

## Author's note: new perceptions —

The story of Guy's day is not a sad story, asking for your sympathy.

Over the years I have discovered that certain things we commonly understand as truths are not necessarily truths at all.

Repeating common misconceptions throughout the day tend to chain us to a "bad day" mentality, instead of uplifting us.

In the next few pages, I am going to introduce new perceptions for all of the italicized and bolded statements from chapter 1, to allow you to view events differently and de-stress your life. After that I will list few of the negative statements from chapters 2, 3, 4, 5, and 6 for you to come up with your own alternate statements.

I've purposely left you plenty of room on these pages to add your own notes and ideas.

# In Chapter 1:

**Why does this have to happen to me today?**
*(p. 7)*

When we make this statement, we are confirming that something bad is happening to us and we must endure it. It also insinuates that someone or something is out to get us. This kind of statement tends to makes us feel like we are being singled out and punished for something.

*Alternate 1:* "I don't like it, but maybe it's a good thing and I might be able to use it to my advantage."

*Alternate 2:* "Okay, I have overslept and I will see what I can do to make up for it."

### How many times do I have to wake her up?
*(p. 8)*

This statement implies that we have no choice in this matter. The thought of not having a choice is stressful because deep down we know that we have a choice in everything we do. When we say that we "have to", our anger arises more from not having a choice than what we are about to do. When we realize that it is our own wish we want to fulfill, we tend to approach these situations much calmer.

*Alternate 1:* "I want to wake her up so we can get going."

*Alternate 2:* "She is rather tired, I will wake her up one more time."

**What's wrong?** *(p. 9)*

We have been told that when someone understands our pain we feel better. In reality we've just added one more person who feels bad and we still haven't gotten to the positive side yet. Saying this tends to confirm the situation as bad and pushes it deeper towards the negative side. Instead of making an accusatory statement and inviting retaliation, we could simply offer assistance.

*Alternate 1:* "Anything I can do?"

*Alternate 2:* "What is it?"

**When you wake up grumpy, you stay grumpy all day.** *(p. 9)*

Often in life, we make blanket statements like this and get stuck with them. This kind of statement does not recognize all the times it didn't come true. Reinforcing the negative side of it only it tends to belittle us and make it harder to change our behavior.

*Alternate 1:* "I do remember, at least once, when I woke up grumpy but managed to have a very good day!"

*Alternate 2:* "I woke up grumpy, but I don't have to stay grumpy all day."

**I hate it when things are not where they should be.** *(p. 10)*

This statement declares that something is really wrong. The truth is simply that something has changed from our routine and an unfamiliar circumstance has occurred. Most of the time we welcome change and actually abhor the sameness of any event. When we scale down the statement a bit and make it a personal issue, it becomes much easier to handle.

*Alternate 1:* "I don't like it when things are not where I like them to be, but it's really not a big deal right now."

*Alternate 2:* "I wish my things were where I expect them to be, but maybe this is an opportunity to change and organize them better."

**I've got to cook breakfast.** *(p. 11)*

This statement eventually leads to, "You have to do it!" When we believe that we have no choice, the next step will be not recognizing that others have choices. If we can't think of any reason why we want to cook breakfast, then not cooking is preferable to eating something someone hated cooking.

*Alternate 1:* "I want to cook breakfast."

*Alternate 2:* "I am going to cook breakfast now!"

**Poor baby...** *(p. 11)*

This statement has the similar effect as "what's wrong" (see above). This statement does not present any solutions and it only confirms the negative aspect of the situation.

*Alternate 1:* "I love you."

*Alternate 2:* "I'm sure you'll figure out something."

**They were always first. Why do I always
have to be last?** *(p. 11)*

Our brain recognizes that we are making a
generalized statement not focused on what's
happening right now. We often feel guilty after
making this kind of statement because deep down,
we know that we are lying. This statement totally
ignores that we have free will and we have always
exercised our free will.

*Alternate 1:* "I usually put them first because
I want to and this time I would like them to
reciprocate if they want to."

*Alternate 2:* "This is where I will ask for their
cooperation."

**What am I complaining about? I should be content.** *(p. 13)*

This statement makes it clear that since I can't exercise my free will, no one can. After mistreating ourselves, we usually demand that others mistreat themselves. We seem to think that when someone else is suffering we feel better. The fact is that when someone else joins in our misery, now we have two people being miserable.

*Alternate 1:* "I sure do love to complain – and that's okay."

*Alternate 2:* "I could complain or I could start being happy about my accomplishments."

**Loser!** *(p. 13)*

Usually we complain when others make derogatory remarks about us, even though we have a choice to let it affect us, or not. However, once we choose to make this kind of statement about ourselves, we are deeply affected by it and will remember it, even for a lifetime.

*Alternate 1:* "I don't like a small part of my life right now, but I am still wonderful!"

*Alternate 2:* "I don't very much like my attitude right now."

## Chapters 2, 3 & 4

Now you take some time to reconsider how the following thoughts and statements from the story affected Guy. Jot down some alternative ways to think and talk about similar events in your life.

"Irene you have to wait." *(p. 16)*

"Gotta go." *(p. 17)*

"It never failed." *(p. 21)*

"Am I the only one who has to stick with a lousy job?" *(p. 26)*

"I am having a bad day." *(p. 32)*

"Come on, stupid! Say something." *(p. 34)*

# Chapter 5 & 6

"Can't I ever get a break?" *(p. 38)*

"How can I be expected to handle everything?" *(p. 42)*

Guy was certain that he was under a big black cloud. *(p. 44)*

"I'm sick and tired of being stuck in this car everyday." *(p. 45)*

"What did I expect? I always get the short end of the stick." *(p. 46)*

"I'm sorry." *(p. 47)*

## Have you heard the news?

Technology has changed the ways business gets done and "leveled the playing field," so that no company, large or small, really has an edge over the others.

Okay, that's not news. Everybody's saying it. But if your company's technology isn't going to be enough, what *is* going to provide that X-factor in the 21st century that will help your company surpass its competition?

People. The "Mental Efficiency" of your people provides the best way to improve the innovative capacity, productivity, and profits of your business. As you've learned from this book, a "bad day" attitude means low mental efficiency.

The **B**usiness **I**mprovement **G**roup (a division of *Mental Efficiency Group, LLC*) applies these mental efficiency principles in its *revolutionary executive coaching program*.

Currently, **BIG** is focusing its program on pharmaceutical company sales departments.

To find out how **BIG** can help your company increase sales and profits through higher mental efficiency of your sales department, contact us at:

### 877-808-0293

or visit us online at:

### www.BigCoach.com